Susan Creek

DOUGLAS WILSON

Susan Creek

veritas
PRESS

For Evangeline Mae Elizabeth,
who arrived the same day the galleys did.

Contents

I.   An Odd Meeting. 9

II.   Word Across the Water 19

III.   John's First Fight 29

IV.   Explanations 39

V.   Pursuit! 47

VI.   "Mr. Whitefield is a Good Man" 57

VII.   Susan Creek 67

VIII.   The Seat of Scoffers 75

IX.   Hanson the Fugitive 85

X.   The Royal Governor 93

XI.   Battle on Prince George's Avenue 103

XII.   Church Across the Waters 111

XIII.   James Gunn at Susan Creek 119

An Odd Meeting

JOHN MONROE TURNED THE GLASGOW CORNER with a quick stride and walked straight into a very surprised woman who had been moving briskly the other way. John jumped back abruptly, startled, and then began picking up a few bundles that she had dropped, apologizing all the while he did so.

The woman was not amused, or annoyed, or anything else that might pertain to John, but just kept looking over her shoulder.

"Come on, mama. We need to hurry." John looked over and was surprised to see a very pretty young girl, about his own age, plucking at her mother's arm. The mother was very pale and white and was coughing a horrible, ragged cough. She was also a pretty woman, about forty years old.

"Yes, yes, we need to go."

"Do you still have it?"

"Yes, right here. *The Golden Sextant* can't be far."

With that the mother and daughter resumed walking quickly down the street toward the harbor. John was mildly annoyed that they had not accepted his apologies—in fact, they had ignored his apologies entirely. But almost immediately, he began to hear his father begin a conversation with him somewhere in his mind, almost out of earshot. "John, a fool shows his annoyance at once. Don't run headlong." As his father's voice faded away, John thought he was going to end the admonition with a characteristic joke, but by this time he was no longer listening. On an irritated whim, he turned and began to follow the women.

This was only the second time that John had been to Glasgow. He was apprenticed to the captain of a tobacco merchant ship and had served him very ably. His family had long experience with the sea, and John's father was a prosperous merchant on the Chesapeake Bay in America. John could have been employed profitably in his father's warehouses, but his father—a kindly man named Thomas Monroe—belonged to that school of thought which held that sons of prosperous merchants ought to have more than a small taste of what it was like to serve in unrewarding positions. "After you have been to sea, you will know what you are doing when you send others to sea in your name, and for the sake of your purse." So John had been apprenticed when he turned sixteen—that had been a year and a half ago—and so it was that he was now walking the streets of Glasgow in search of some mutton and ale in the late spring of 1747. He was grateful for his experience at sea, but he was also ready for something else. And sometimes he wondered if the length of his apprenticeship decided on by his father had not slowed down his ambitions too much. Still, as he had once thought to himself, he would do it again, but he would not do it over.

But now he was walking back toward his ship, not really wanting to, but keeping the two women in sight. He knew that what he was doing made no real sense, but he was an impulsive (and adventurous, romantic and chivalrous) young man. He was not as impulsive as he had been several years before, but still enough to walk down a Glasgow street in a direction contrary to his earlier plans. Because the street was so crowded, John only had to stay about fifty feet back to keep from being noticed. He did not know why he was following them, but it seemed to him at the time to be a mixture of annoyance and a desire to make amends somehow. He was just about to give it up as a ridiculous venture and return to his search for an inn that kept better victuals than could be had back on the ship. But just as he started to turn back, looking over his shoulder as he did so, he stopped suddenly.

An officer in his majesty's service in a distinguished red coat had stepped quickly out of an alley that the two women

were passing and took the mother firmly by the arm. There
was no one else with him. John stopped, and he started to walk
slowly back toward the confrontation. His mouth was suddenly dry, and he could feel his heart pounding in his ears. The
officer was intently whispering to the woman, and she was
replying and gesticulating with her free hand. The daughter
looked as though she was imploring the man to let them go,
and as John came closer he heard the mother saying, "... but I
don't have it!" The officer hissed something in reply that John
could not hear, and John, just like the officer, was sure that she
did have it.

To the end of his life, John could never explain what he did
next. He did not know these women, and he did not know if the
officer was a good man or a wicked man. He did not know if
he was trying to get something back that belonged to him, or if
he was trying to rob the women of something that was theirs.
He did not know anything except that he had bumped into a
woman trying to get away from someone, and here, apparently,
was that someone. How he chose between them, he never knew
for certain. But he did admit to himself later that the girl was a
lot prettier than the officer.

John was only about fifteen feet away by this time. He broke
into a run, and by the time he reached them he was running at
full speed, straight at the officer. He remembered few things
about this later, but one of his vivid memories was the daughter's eyes getting very round as she saw him careening toward

the officer's right shoulder. The man was a soldier, hard and massive, and John was surprised afterwards that he had been able to knock him over, sprawling on top of him. In his surprise, the officer had let go of the mother, and John shouted at them to run. "Go! Go!"

John jumped back to his feet, turned on his heel and ran as fast as he could back up the street, away from the harbor, hoping that the officer would change his mind and think that *he* had it, whatever it was. He stopped at a corner, just before he turned it, and looked back down the street. He could see flashes of red through the crowd, and he laughed out loud. The soldier was following him and not the women. John was light on his feet, and very confident about his ability to outrun the officer. And so that is what he did, running up the street for about half a mile. Before he turned another corner in order to circle back toward the harbor, he stopped again and looked back down the street. No sign of red at all.

Now all he had to do was find *The Golden Sextant.* He briefly played with the idea of just heading back to his ship in case the officer had gotten a good glimpse of him, but by now the spirit of adventure was on him completely. He needed to find what he supposed was an inn. It was certainly *named* like an inn.

Darkness was approaching as John walked slowly back toward the harbor. Every time he came to a cross street, he would stop at the corner and look to the right toward the street where the confrontation had happened. Occasionally, he saw red-coated soldiers but this was not at all unusual, and they did not appear to be looking for anyone.

When he had made his way about a mile toward the water, he began asking for directions to *The Golden Sextant*. The first three people he asked had no idea, and the fourth thought it was somewhere near the "old Presbyterian church." Every block or so John would ask again, and finally he found someone who gave him some clear directions, somewhat confidently.

John caught a glimpse of a golden sextant hanging above the street before he could make out the words. As he walked up to the front door of the tavern—for it was a tavern—he naively thought that he would meet the women, receive their proper thanks, and then make his way back to the ship, his small adventure concluded. He had never been so completely wrong in his life.

It took a moment for his eyes to adjust to the candlelight, and when they did, he saw the daughter sitting at a table against the back wall. Apart from her table, the tavern was empty. A man was sitting with her, apparently the proprietor of the tavern, holding her hand and obviously comforting her. She saw John and dully waved him over. As he approached, he saw that her eyes were red from crying, and he pulled up a bench, puzzled.

"Her mother has died," the proprietor said. "She had a coughing fit just after she got here."

John sat bolt upright, surprised and shocked, and stammered out his condolences. The girl nodded, miserably.

The proprietor of the inn—his name was James Gunn—continued to talk with the girl. "I dinna think your circumstances are changed at all. Or if they are, it's all to the worse. The men after you are *still* after you, and you must still leave the country immediately. I will see that your mother gets a decent Christian burial. You have to leave and take all that your mother had."

"I am here on a ship from America," John volunteered. "We sail for home tomorrow, at high tide. We have some berths for passengers."

"What is the ship?" Mr. Gunn asked.

"The *Sea Breeze*," John said.

"She has a good captain," Mr. Gunn said. "A Mr. Wainwright, is that correct?"

John nodded, impressed.

Mr. Gunn looked across the table at the daughter, who thought for a moment, and then nodded reluctantly. "I was ready for mama to die," she said. "She had consumption bad. But I was not expecting it so soon, or so suddenly."

"But what do we know about you, young man?" Mr. Gunn looked gruffly across the table at John with a thick Scots stare. "Why should I entrust this young lass to you?"

"You know of me about what I know of you. But it appears that providence has thrown us together. I am willing to help, provided you are doing nothing wicked or unlawful."

Mr. Gunn chuckled and said, "Aye. Well said." He got up and disappeared into a back room and came back out a moment later with a brace of pistols and some gold coins. He dropped them all on the table in front of John, who stared at them in consternation. It was one thing to run into an officer and knock him down—without knowing why—but it was quite another to be armed for a conflict about which he knew nothing. "What are the coins for?" he asked.

"For her passage. The *Sea Breeze* is not carrying passengers free, are they?"

John shook his head.

"Do you have everything with you?" Mr. Gunn asked the young woman. She nodded. He turned to John. "Are you willing to take her back to your ship now?" He said *yes,* and they all stood up slowly.

When they were outside in the gloaming, she turned to John and said, "Thank you for what you did. My name is Jenny. Jenny Geddes."

"My name is John," John said. "You're welcome. I am very sorry about your mother. The ship is this way."

Word Across the Water

THEY ARRIVED AT THE SHIP SAFELY THAT evening, and Jenny had no problem acquiring a berth. The captain looked at John curiously when they arrived, and John had to put up with some raucous teasing from some of the crew, but once she had secured her passage, John had disappeared below decks and did not see her again until they had been out to sea for a day.

A brisk spring wind kept their sails full, and the bow pointed eagerly west. After they had been out at sea for three days, the lookout shouted out that he saw three sets of masts, all sails furled, out on the horizon. It was early on a Sunday, and the *Sea Breeze* rapidly overtook them.

Captain Wainwright paced up and down the deck

nervously, and periodically he would raise his glass, trying to calculate what the three ships were doing. There did not appear to be any danger, but it was still strange to find three ships just bobbing about. At the captain's orders, the *Sea Breeze* tacked to come within hailing distance, and as they did so, John could hear a faint voice coming over the water.

The captain raised his glass again, and this time he lowered it with an exclamation. "By thunder, a preacher!" He handed the glass to John, who had been standing behind him ready to be sent on errands. "A *preacher!*"

"All hands on deck!"

"All hands on deck, aye!"

John turned and saw the crew scrambling to obey the captain's order. Within a few minutes, the entire crew was assembled on the afterdeck, lined up in three disciplined lines. Their disciplined and immediate response to the captain's order provided an apparent contrast with some of their very colorful garb—wide leather belts, homespun shirts and the occasional earring. Some of the men looked quite piratical. The few passengers—there were a handful besides Jenny—stood behind the crew curiously. The passengers, I am afraid to say, were dressed far more respectably.

"Mates," the captain said, "button up your shirts. *We* are going to church."

The *Sea Breeze* gradually came in closer to the three ships, and John could plainly hear the words of the black-robed preacher standing on a wooden box near the after rail. At the captain's order, their sails were furled, and they began to drift about fifty yards starboard of the nearest ship. The preacher was on the middle ship, and his voice boomed over the water. John had never heard a voice like it. It was rolling and full, like the ocean beneath them, and John almost could feel the weight of his vowels. He could see the crews of the other ships clustered around him, seated on the deck.

> *But before I come directly to this, give me leave to premise a caution or two. And the first is, that I take it for granted you believe religion to be an inward thing; you believe it to be a work in the heart, a work wrought in the soul by the power of the Spirit of God. If you do not believe this, you do not believe your Bibles. If you do not believe this, though you have got your Bibles in your hand, you hate the Lord Jesus Christ in your heart; for religion is everywhere represented in Scripture as the work of God in the heart. "The kingdom of God is within us," says our Lord; and, "He is not a Christian who is one outwardly; but he is a Christian who is one inwardly." If any of you place religion in outward things, I shall not perhaps please you this morning . . .*

John had grown up in St. Anne's church in Annapolis, and his parents had catechized him faithfully. He was not hearing anything new in what the preacher was saying, but he was certainly hearing it in a fresh way. The vicar at St. Anne's was a kindly man, but somewhat helpless outside the pulpit, and only slightly better than that inside in the pulpit. He frequently read sermons that others had written many years before, and John was not always entirely sure that he even understood what he was reading. At the same time, John still felt bad for feeling this way because the vicar really was a very nice man. One time John's father had joked that the vicar could preach about as well as a pile of wet rope, and John had laughed out loud. His mother had shushed them both, but then had smiled in spite of herself. She was always shushing his father that way.

> *. . . I can do nothing without sin; and, as one expresseth it, my repentance wants to be repented of, and my tears to be washed in the precious blood of my dear Redeemer. Our best duties are as so many splendid sins.*

John was leaning on the rail, listening intently. *Splendid* sins. That's what it was, splendid sinning. One time, his father had threatened to start taking the family to the Presbyterian meeting house outside of town, and his parents had quite a discussion about it. But St. Anne's really was a beautiful place, and John loved to go there when no one else was around, just to sit and think and pray. He loved the silence and the glory of the sanctuary's lines. The Presbyterian meeting house was a

converted stable, and the Monroes were a well-respected family in Annapolis. Going there would not be a secret thing in Annapolis society at all. And yet, John knew that his father and mother were both sympathetic with the preaching outside of town, and he could tell from the books they bought and read that their sympathies were well-informed. And yet, for the time being, they all remained at St. Anne's—though his father commented on it more often than his mother did. One time, as they walked home from church, Thomas Monroe had looked at John and said, "Son, there are only two consolations in this sinful world. One is the perfections of Christ. The other is the imperfections of Christians." John had laughed, his mother tried not to smile, and nothing more was said.

. . . you must not build upon a work within you, but always come out of yourselves to the righteousness of Jesus Christ without you; you must be always coming as poor sinners to draw water out of the wells of salvation; you must be forgetting the things that are behind, and be continually pressing forward to the things that are before. My dear friends, you must keep up a tender, close walk with the Lord Jesus Christ.

Now John knew that he was a Christian. But as the preacher drew his sermon to a close, John felt himself mysteriously drawn to some point of decision. He felt convicted that he had been lax in his reading of his prayer book, the one his mother had given him. And he knew his father would ask him about his Bible reading when he got home again. He resolved to make sure he could give them both a good report. At the same time, the preacher was making it very clear that Jesus Christ did not come to make nice people nicer. John felt quite sure that nice people becoming nicer was one of the splendid sins that the preacher had so roundly condemned. But even though the words of the preacher struck him powerfully, so that he felt pierced in his heart, at the same time, John felt himself strangely encouraged. He did not know how to explain it, but fortunately there was no one there that he had to explain it to.

He bowed his head respectfully while the preacher was saying the last prayer and benediction. He lifted up his head after the prayer and saw Captain Wainwright lift his hands to his mouth to shout across the water.

"Our many thanks to you, and to your minister!" A faint cry drifted back across the water, nowhere near as powerful as the voice of the preacher. "You are most welcome, and Mr. Whitefield sends his regards."

Mr. Whitefield! John's mouth dropped open. He had heard his parents talk of Mr. Whitefield often—if only all Anglican ministers preached like he did, there would be no need of the Presbyterians outside the town. And here he had heard Mr. Whitefield preach without knowing who it was. Yet at the same time, even though he did not know who was preaching, he had felt the force of his authority. Mr. Whitefield's reputation was certainly well-deserved. And here John had found him, out in the middle of the ocean. He was delighted, and he wondered what his parents would say when he told them about it.

The sailors were all variously affected. Most of them had simply returned to their tasks when the service was done, but others moved slowly around the deck, appearing deep in thought. Several men went below decks immediately, and John could hear them beginning to blaspheme as soon as they thought the captain couldn't hear them. The passengers responded as most of the crew had, and John noticed Jenny standing off by herself next to the opposite rail. He walked up to her slowly, and saw that she had been crying. Unwiped tears were still on her cheeks. She just stood motionless as he walked up.

"Jenny? Are you all right?" At this she just nodded.

And so he asked, "Was it the sermon?" She nodded again, and after a moment, she spoke slowly. "I have never heard anything like that before. Most Sundays my mother would take me to the old greystone kirk near our house, but I never heard anything there but very learned mumbling. One minister we had would creak when he walked."

"What kind of church was it?" John asked.

Jenny laughed. "Scotland, remember? Presbyterian. But I hear that this Mr. Whitefield is an Anglican. How wonderful it must be to hear preaching like that all the time."

John said nothing, but was musing to himself what an

odd world it was. His parents were wishing they could hear Presbyterian preaching, and here was Jenny, who apparently had had her fill of it. So John stood decently off to the side and tried hard not to think about how pretty she was.

"What did you think of the sermon?" she suddenly asked.

"I believe him," he said simply.

"So do I," she said.

"What did you think about what he said about being a Christian inwardly?" she asked. "I had never heard that before."

"I thought he was right. But I am not sure it always looks the same, and I think that some enthusiasts think that it does. I talked to my father about this once, and what he told me helped me a great deal. He likes the revival preachers mostly, but he said some of them are barking at the moon. Not Mr. Whitefield though." At this, John's voice became more serious and solemn. He moved to the gunwale and hopped slightly to sit on the rail. As he did so, the ship took an unexpected lurch, and John toppled over backwards and into the sea.

John's First Fight

THE SHIP WAS NOT UNDER SAIL, AND THE DAY was relatively calm, so they had no trouble getting John back on board. A rope was thrown down to him, and as he clambered back on board, over the rail, he flushed deeply under the crew's jibing and catcalls. He did not know why, but he was very irritated, and when Jenny asked him if he was all right, he just nodded curtly. After a moment of shaking himself off, he stomped down below to change into dry clothing.

Everything seemed wrong to him. He had heard a wonderful sermon, and he had taken it to heart. He had been able to speak with Jenny and thought that perhaps she might *not* be taking him for a fool, when he had to go and flip backward off the rail and into the deep, blue sea. He was completely humiliated and in a dangerous mood.

When he came topside later that day, he was glad to see that the deck was largely empty. One sailor stood watch at the helm, and another stood beside him, keeping him company. John walked slowly back to the stern of the ship in order to stand at one of his favorite places, so that he might watch the wake of the ship curl and boil and return to the ocean. He just wanted to think.

As he walked by the helmsman, he did not see the two exchange glances. The man at the helm shook his head *no*, but his friend—whose name was Curtis—seemed insistent. They whispered back and forth for a moment, and then Curtis turned and spoke loudly to John.

"Hey, laddie. Tell us about your lady friend!"

John did not turn and just shook his head.

"Well, maybe we should tell you about *her* then."

John's shoulders stiffened, and he continued to pretend that he was not listening. But it was obvious that he was listening.

"Correct that, laddie. I don't know about her. Jenny, that's her name, ain't it? But I do know about her mother. D'ye want to hear about her mother?"

At this, John stood up and turned around. His forehead was red, and his cheeks were flushed with anger. "No."

Curtis grinned widely. "Only one way to keep me from talking, laddie. You see, one time last year . . ."

At this, John roared and lunged toward Curtis, but in his

anger he did not move intelligently. Curtis, who was one of
the sailors who had been blaspheming after hearing Mr.
Whitefield, was agitated and looking for a fight. He calcu-
lated everything perfectly. The sermon earlier in the day had
an effect on him, too, one that he did not care to think about.
Fighting was a good way to think about something else.

When John ran at Curtis, he had no other thought in his
mind other than his anger and his desire to do something. He
was completely shocked when Curtis, who had been plotting
the fight beforehand, threw a right fist into his face, which
knocked him on to his back. John lay on the deck, stunned for
a moment. In the background, he could hear the helmsman
trying to restrain his friend. "That's enough now, Jack . . ."

But when John's scattered senses came back to him, the
hot anger was completely gone. In its place was a cold wrath,
and a deep sense that he was involved with a kind of situation
he had never been in before. He stood slowly to his feet, and
approached Curtis warily this time, his fists up in front of him.

Jack Curtis was about ten years older than John, and he was
about twenty pounds heavier. John thought coldly to himself
that Curtis was probably going to thrash him, and that his only
goal should simply be to acquit himself well. But even with his
hot anger gone, John was vaguely aware that his motives were
mixed, and that in part he was fighting because he had fallen
into the water, or perhaps because Jenny's mother had not
received his apology, or perhaps because he had completely

misunderstood Mr. Whitefield's sermon, thinking that he was a nice person because he knew that being a nice person was not enough. There was more than enough in Curtis's taunts to fight over—he had no right to speak about Jenny's mother that way. But John circled around the older sailor, fists in front of him, and he knew that he was not going to be able to fight with that abandon that comes with a clean conscience. He was going to fight, and he was going to do the best he could, but his thoughts were all a jumble. And he was still very angry. His father had once told him that there was always a deeper right than being right. But now he was only in the right one way. And he had to fight anyway.

John was very quick on his feet, and so he was able to strike Curtis on the face, but not very hard. But Curtis just grinned at him again. "So, you can slap like a girl."

With that, John stepped in to swing at Curtis with all that he had, and Curtis just slapped away his punch like he wasn't even trying. John did not retreat and took several heavy swings in quick succession. One of his left jabs caught Curtis on the nose, and John noted with satisfaction that he had drawn first blood. But Curtis was a strong man and had been a sailor of the main for fifteen years, and with his first blow he knocked John down again, sprawling on his back.

John got up again, and this time he just charged. He wrapped his arms around Curtis, and they both toppled to the deck. By this time, the commotion attracted a good portion

of the crew, and they stood in a tight circle around the fight-
ers, cheering them both on. The crew members knew nothing about the origins of the fight and were just happy with
the entertainment, and so they lustily cheered both of the
combatants on.

In close quarters, John was taking the worst of it. He had
longer arms than Curtis and could not effectively draw back
in order to swing. Curtis was short and stocky, and every blow
to John's ribs knocked wind out of him. Curtis was an experienced fighter, and he knew that blows to the body took a lot
more out of a man than blows to the head, and he just kept
pummeling away. John was finding it difficult to breath, both
because of the blows to the ribs and because of the exertion of
fighting. He was not doing well at all, and he knew it. He had
not expected to win, but he *had* expected to do better than he
was doing.

He rolled quickly away from Curtis on the deck, and
lurched to his feet. Curtis got to his knees, and they both faced
each other for a few moments, breathing heavily. Curtis slowly
got to his feet, and John ran at him with all his strength, and
delivered a blow that had everything in it that John had left in
him. He struck Curtis full in the face, and the sailor fell over
backwards like a tree. John had fallen to his knees afterwards,
and was facing the deck on all fours, trying to get air into his
lungs. But this last blow, although it had knocked Curtis over,
had also made him angry for the first time. Up to this point, he

was just entertaining himself, but now he had lost his temper with John and fell upon him savagely. John had no more to fight with, and he lost consciousness with Curtis raining blows upon his head.

As soon as John went limp, the rest of the crew, which was made up of a decent sort for the most part, pulled Curtis off, and pinned his arms behind him. Several of them knelt down beside John to attend to him, and this was the scene on the afterdeck when Captain Wainwright walked up. He took everything in at a glance and stared coldly around at the crew. "Who was here when this started?"

"Aye, Cap'n." The helmsman raised his hand.

"Who started it?"

The helmsman just stared for a moment, swallowed a couple times and then said, "Jack did, Cap'n." The captain looked at Curtis angrily. "That true, Curtis?"

"Aye, Cap'n."

"Take Monroe below decks to his bunk, and tend to him until he comes to. Tie Curtis to the mast, and ten lashes, smart and quick. Then take him below."

When John came to his senses, all he could hear was moaning. At first, he thought he was the one doing it, but after a moment his head cleared, and he could hear that it was someone else. Later on he found out it was Curtis, on the far side of the crew's quarters, just fresh from the lash.

He tried to move in his bunk and gasped in pain. Some of his ribs were broken, he was sure, and the left side of his face was swollen. He tried to open his left eye, but he was unsure if he had done so. He couldn't see anything out of it. He tried to lick his lips, but it didn't seem like his tongue could move. He was thirsty enough to spit cotton.

"You awake?"

John could not see anything but croaked an answer.

"You want some water?"

John croaked again, and a moment later he could feel a pewter tumbler pressing his lips. He greedily drank what he could and even enjoyed the water running down his chin.

"Thank you," he said. "Who is it?"

"Henry," came the voice.

"Thank you, Henry," John said.

"You are most welcome, you stupid, little puppy," Henry said.

"May I have another drink?"

"All you want. And the barrel is not that far away."

John took another deep drink and then lay back in his bunk. After stretching out as best he could, he carefully checked all his limbs. He moved both feet and then his legs.

After that he successfully moved both arms and clenched and released both fists. Everything still worked. His arms and hands were very sore, but he thought they would be back to normal in a day or two. He reached up and gingerly touched his face. He flinched as he did so and decided that he had learned enough about his face.

"I don't blame you," Henry's voice said. "It looks bad enough without poking it. I have never seen quite so puffy a head."

All that was left for John was finding out about his ribs. "Can you help me, Henry? I think some ribs are broke. Could you feel up and down? Gentle, gentle."

Henry ran his hand softly up one side and down the other, gently pressing as he went. The painful ribs were on his left side, and it seemed there were three of them that were broken.

"Stove right in," Henry said cheerfully. "Looks like you have some bunk time coming."

John got another drink and then laid his head back cautiously. He felt all right as long as he did not move, and it was generally easy to not move. As he lay on his back, his thoughts wandered here and there, and he began to reflect on the day he had had. It had begun wonderfully, listening to Mr. Whitefield preach. But then he had fallen in the water, and then he had fought with Curtis . . .

John suddenly lurched up and then fell back in pain. Henry, startled, grabbed at John's hand. "What? What is it?"

"The Lord's Day! I was fighting on the Lord's Day!"

"The good Lord wanted you to wait a day? He wants all good Christians to get in their fights on Monday?"

"That's not it. It's always a sin—at least the way I was doing it. But on the Lord's Day! That's sacrilege."

"Suit yourself, Johnny. Doing theology is as good a way to spend time down here while you are fixing up your ribs as anything else. Keeps your mind off the mending so's you don't mess that up, too. Is there anything else you want? I was just told to stay down here until you came to."

"No," John said. "Yes. Tell the captain I am very sorry, and I will be back in his service as his cabin boy as soon as I can. And can I have one more drink before you go? How is Curtis?"

"Never you mind about Curtis. The captain would have your hide if more fighting broke out down here."

"No, no fighting. I just need to apologize to him also."

"I don't think he is in a frame of mind to receive visitors just now. Maybe tomorrow."

"Maybe tomorrow."

Explanations

JOHN SLEPT SOUNDLY THAT NIGHT, FLAT ON HIS
back. He woke only once during the night, and that was just
for a few brief moments. After he woke up late in the morning,
the crew's quarters were empty again. He lay there for about
a half an hour, enjoying the sensations of not moving and the
very different sensations of running his tongue around the inside of his mouth, feeling for loose teeth.

After a short time, Henry stopped in on him again. "You'll
be wanting more water, I'll be bound."

John nodded weakly, took another drink, and thanked
Henry again. "You hungry?" Henry asked.

"Yes, I am. But I am afraid if I eat anything, my teeth will fall
out. I need to wait a bit longer."

"Aye. There is wisdom. Finally."

"Thank you, Henry."

"There is one other thing," Henry said. "The lass you brought on board? She asked the captain if she could come down to see you. He said yes, if you did not mind. Do you mind?"

John had not thought of this at all. He tried to pull himself up in bed and tried to assume a dignified posture. "How do I look?"

Henry shook his head. "Awful. I saw worse one time, thirty years ago in London."

"Maybe I shouldn't."

"She really wants to see you. I wouldn't argue with her. Besides, she's the one that has to look at the sight. You don't need to worry about it."

John was thinking furiously, trying to find a way out. There was no way out. Finally, reluctantly, he nodded. "She can come down."

Once John gave permission for her to come see him, he began rehearsing little speeches in his mind. How was he going to explain this? What was he going to say? It was about fifteen minutes before she came, and John was turning everything over in his mind, again and again.

But when she arrived, he said nothing, and neither did she. She just stood by his bunk, took his hand and stood quietly. They both knew that they had to talk, but neither one felt like talking. But after about ten minutes, John finally took a deep breath and said, "I have a confession."

She said, "I have one too. But you can go first."

John tried to look at her through his right eye and tried to assemble his thoughts. "I got into this fight because I was a fool. My pride was offended because I fell overboard and because you and your mother did not receive my apologies the evening I ran into you. I was proud that I understood Mr. Whitefield's sermon, and probably a host of other splendid sins beside. I was trying to impress you, and everything I did just made me more of a fool. So when Curtis said what he did, I had my excuse for fighting. And it would have been a noble fight if that had been my only reason. But in my case, it wasn't. That is my confession. I think that is everything."

Jenny looked at him carefully. "I think you are very brave and very kind. My confession is a little bit harder, but I have to tell you because I need someone's help, and you are the only one I can trust. Is there anyone else down here?"

"Just Curtis at the other end of the quarters. But I am sure he is asleep. He stopped groaning some time ago."

Jenny lowered her voice. "What Curtis said about my mother was . . . was true. And that is how we got into so much trouble. My mother had some . . . some gentlemen friends in the English army. About six months ago, she had a dispute with one of them over money—he was the one you knocked down in Glasgow. He owed her quite a bit of money. So she took some of his papers one day for security. She thought it was an innocent way to make an acquaintance pay what he owed. But instead, he became furious and threatened to kill us both if the papers were not returned to him immediately. My mother was very frightened, and had gotten very sick by this time. She went to where she had hidden the papers and looked them over carefully. And when she read them, she discovered that Major Hanson—that is his name—must be a spy for the French king. The papers are all about a place in America, and a man who is working for the French there. If the papers get to the English, then Major Hanson will surely be hanged. Our only friend was James Gunn—he is my mother's cousin. We have been running and hiding ever since then."

"Why don't you just give the papers to the English authorities?"

"I asked mother many times to do just that. But it is far more complicated than that. James Gunn was our counselor, and he fought in the '45 with Bonnie Prince Charlie against the English, and that was just two years ago. There is no love lost between him and the English at all. But he loves the French no better, and he hates traitors worst of all. 'Traitors brought down the Bonnie Prince,' he said, 'and all traitors to everyone should all be sent to the same place right off, so they could commiserate with the devil and Judas." At this Jenny scowled just like James Gunn would have done.

"So I still don't understand," John asked. "Why didn't he go along with turning the papers over then?"

"Because he had fought very bravely at Culloden, and he is still a wanted man. The English have suppressed the clans and are driving all the Scots men, at least those with backbone, out of Scotland. James Gunn is moving to America as soon as he can. But until then, he has a price on his head. He can't just walk up to the English and deliver them a traitor. They would say he delivered them *two* traitors."

"And your mother . . .?"

"She didn't want to do anything like that by herself. And Mr. Gunn advised against that too. Once she revealed herself to army headquarters, she would have no way to hide from Major Hanson, and she would have no idea who were his friends there, or perhaps even his fellow traitors. So all we could do is run and hide, and try to save up enough money for passage to America."

"What were your plans for America?"

"We didn't know. That is why I needed to talk to you. James Gunn is sure they are still after me and that someone will follow us to America. The only choices I can think of are to throw the papers overboard, take a new name in America and try to disappear, or else study the papers and try to figure out what they are about and try to help the English against the French in America. That should not be as hard as doing it in Scotland. But it still might be impossible."

"And you have these papers on board with you?"

"Yes," Jenny said, miserably.

"Do you have any relatives or friends in America? We are going to Annapolis, just south of Baltimore."

Jenny shook her head. "No. My only family is Mr. Gunn. He will follow as soon as he can. He has to sell *The Golden Sextant.*"

"Has he seen the papers?"

"No. He knows about them and what's in them. But my mother kept them carefully hidden. After she passed away, I offered to give them to Mr. Gunn. But he said *no.* He thought they needed to get out of Scotland."

In spite of himself, John felt his heart starting to rise within him. First, he was glad that the man he had knocked down in the street was a wicked man. And second, he began to get excited about a possible adventure, a true adventure. And third, he was mostly excited that Jenny had trusted him with all her troubles.

"Thank you for trusting me," he said.

"I knew that I could after I heard how you fought Curtis."

"Even though I was sinning my head off?"

Jenny smiled at him. "Yes, but they were splendid sins."

They were quiet for a few moments more. Then Jenny asked, "What shall we do?"

John said, "Well, I have to get my ribs back. We are at sea for several more weeks, and I will have a few days to lie here and try to think up a plan. We have to think this through carefully. And after we are back in Annapolis, we can get counsel from my father. My indentures are up after this trip, and I don't need to sail anywhere soon. We can take stock of our situation there, and see what God gives us."

They were interrupted by Henry, who came down to see if John wanted help in walking around the crews' quarters. With a great deal of trouble, he got John out of his bunk, and they walked through the quarters twice. The second time through, they stopped by Curtis' bunk, where he was lying on his stomach, barely awake. He saw them stop, and opened his eyes further.

"Curtis," John said, "I owe you an apology. Will you forgive me for fighting with you the way I did?"

"I've been thinking," Curtis said. "I shouldn't have done nothing either. I'm sorry. The cap'n helped me see things this way."

Pursuit!

T HE SEA BREEZE ARRIVED AT THE MOUTH OF the Chesapeake several weeks later, and slowly began to sail north, tacking back and forth. Jenny looked out at the Eastern Shore wistfully. "It's lovely," she said. "A new world."

"My town is on the other shore," John said. He was now able to move about, if he did so carefully, and had been able to resume his duties with the captain about a week before. The captain had chided him mildly for having lost a week of labor, but then had forgiven him quite gracefully.

John had only returned from sea to Annapolis once before, and he felt the same way now as he had the first time. His chest was tight, he had a lump in his throat, and he found himself looking off the port bow every five minutes. The bay seemed to

crawl reluctantly under the hull of the ship, and John impatiently felt as though time had gone off somewhere else.

"Do your parents live in Annapolis?" Jenny asked.

"Yes," John said. "They live in a great manor on the other
side of the governor's mansion."

Jenny's eyes got wide. "They live in a manor? Your parents
are rich? But that means that you are rich. Why are you a cabin
boy?" Her questions just tumbled out.

John laughed. He had never thought of his parents as rich,
but he supposed that they were. "My father believes that all
boys need to know the meaning of work. He has told me that
often enough, and I know he believes it."

"But I can't go to your house like this!" Jenny looked down at
her dress, which was mended and patched in many places. "I
didn't know your parents were rich!"

John laughed again. "You don't need to worry about that.
But I should explain things to them before you come to the
house. There is an inn right near where we live, a place called
Reynold's Inn. I am going to take you there and then go see them
and tell them about you. Then I'll come right back and get you.
It is just a few streets away."

Jenny nodded, still unhappy about having to meet his parents looking like a scullery maid. She had *been* a scullery maid
before, but she liked John, and she didn't want to meet his parents that way. But there was nothing to be done.

Late that day, the ship came to the mouth of the Severn

River and began to work its way up to the docks. John stood happily near the bow, and spotted the spire of St. Anne's and the dome of the capitol building that was just going up. The sailors swarmed over the rigging and brought the ship into port with an expert touch. The ship finally touched the dock on the port side, as gently as a bird settling into a nest. The lines were quickly tied off, and the deck was restored shipshape in just a matter of minutes. Captain Wainwright finished issuing the orders for docking and looked with satisfaction at the work of the crew.

"Men," he said. "There is no sense in off-loading cargo to-night. Tomorrow it is, and you know who has the duty." The crew roared their approval and began making their way down the gangplank. John and Jenny waited until most of them were gone. John was hanging back in order to thank the captain—his indentures were up, and he had all his belongings in a tuck sack slung over his shoulder. When he had said his thanks and farewell, he and Jenny made their way down the gangway and up the street toward *Reynold's Inn.*

They found their way there easily, with Jenny looking around curiously at this new town in a new world. When they came to the front door of the inn, John had Jenny sit on a bench near the front door. "I will be back in about fifteen minutes," he said.

As he walked toward his house, he found his pace quickening. His father would be home from the warehouses, and he knew that his mother would be there. All sorts of things pushed their way into his mind. He needed to tell them about Jenny first, of course, and some of the difficulties. He would tell his father everything about it later. And he would have to tell them why he was limping, and that he had gotten into a fight the same day he had heard Mr. Whitefield preach. And then he would come back for Jenny.

His homecoming was even better than the last one. His mother (her name was Jane) saw him coming up the street and ran out the front door, calling his father as she came. When John saw her coming, in spite of his injuries, he vaulted the iron gate at the front of their house, and picked up his mother and swung her around. "Oh, it's good to see you!" they both said, and then both laughed.

His father came around the side of the house, wiping his hands on an old cloth. He had been back in the kennels with his hunting dogs when he heard his wife calling him. "Thomas, Thomas! John's home!" There were hugs and handshakes everywhere, and John laughed, and his parents laughed. Several of the servants gathered round, all of them gladly welcoming the young master home. But after five minutes of this, John remembered himself, and told his parents he had to speak with them privately about something urgent.

At this, they went inside to his father's study, and Thomas Monroe carefully closed the door. John quickly gave them the circumstances that Jenny was in, and asked if he could

bring her to stay with them. His parents both seemed concerned, his mother more than his father, but both of them readily agreed. "I will have Jema prepare the guest room right now," his mother said.

"I will be right back then," said John, and out the door he went. He made his way back to *Reynold's Inn*, with his hands in his pockets, and he was whistling carelessly. But as he walked out onto Church Circle and walked toward the inn he was puzzled that Jenny was not sitting on the bench where he had left her. He walked up to the porch of the inn and stared at the bench for a moment. He looked back toward St. Anne's, and he saw a young woman hastening away. He was sure it was Jenny. What could she be doing?

He turned back to go into the inn to ask the proprietor if she had left a message. If she had not, then he could just chase her down. But why should he have to do that? He began to stomp up the stairs, annoyed with her for running off, and looked up just as he got to the top stair. And when he looked up, he was completely astonished to see Major Hanson come out the front door of the inn. Their eyes met, and there was instant and mutual recognition. Major Hanson was not in uniform, and he had a nasty-looking companion, one who looked as though he would kill you for a shilling.

John gasped and had only three thoughts that jumbled in his mind all together. The first was to run as he had never run before. The second was to run away from where Jenny was headed, wherever that was. She must have seen Hanson go into the inn, and he had somehow had missed her. The third thing was to run in a direction away from his house. But he knew Annapolis, and he suspected that these two gentlemen did not. Nevertheless, they were obviously motivated to learn. John thought all this before anyone moved, and then he clattered back down the wooden steps and took to his heels.

Both men were right after him, and this time John did not have the head start that he had had in Glasgow. Not toward the harbor, that is where Jenny seemed to be going. There were clusters of buildings over near King Williams College, and numerous alleys and ornamental gardens over there. He knew that he could probably win a footrace, but he did not want to do that. He needed to lose them completely, so that they would stop running and start hunting. It was also late in the day, and the twilight would be on them soon enough. John looked over his shoulder and saw that he had put about twenty-five yards between them.

He continued to run, looking over his shoulder every time he turned a corner. He was coming to the part of town where he had spent many summer evenings as a small boy, playing at hoops or hide and seek, and he almost laughed out loud. You never know what lessons you might need to remember the most, he thought. He recalled a hiding place that was back behind the Hammond house, a place that he had found when he was eleven and which all the other children had pronounced as "cheating." It was *that* good a hiding place.

It was an elm tree with a double trunk that had grown up next to a shed. There was a hollow "V" on the backside of those trunks, one that you could crawl up into and completely disappear. John was confident that he had enough of a lead to get into that place before the two men turned the corner of that alley, and then he would have still more time to get his breathing under control and his heart to stop pounding. The hole was smaller than he remembered it, but he still fit in there nicely.

He was completely ready for them to pass by when he heard the oyster shells of the alley crunching under some feet. If it was Hanson and his companion, they were no longer running. When the footsteps came near the elm, they suddenly stopped. John wondered if they were giving up, or if they had guessed at his hiding place. But he was not really worried about that—the hiding place was *that* good.

After a moment, one of the voices, a very gruff one, spoke. "Well, he just flew away."

"Aye, but we'll get him soon enow." John guessed that this was Hanson.

"How's that you figure?"

"This is not a city like Glasgow or London. We'll just ask around at the docks. He had to have come in today or yesterday."

"D'ye think the wench is with him?"

"Aye. Why would he come here without her?"

"We have to find them tomorrow."

Hanson replied, "That's true enough. I have to meet with the marquis on Friday, at Susan Creek. He will want those papers. Without them, I have some things to give him, but not enough to make him really happy. With them, he will have enough to persuade five tribes to join with the French against the English."

The first man grunted, apparently in satisfaction. He approved of slaughtering settlers on the frontier. But not for political reasons—he just approved of slaughter.

"And just to encourage you in your work tomorrow, if the English get those papers, there is enough there to bring the both of us to swing."

With that, they both began to walk again, and John listened to the crunch of the shells until they faded completely. He then waited for dark, slithered out of his hiding place, and walked thoughtfully home.

"Mr. Whitefield is a Good Man"

LATER THAT EVENING, THOMAS MONROE walked down to the *Sea Breeze* to see if Jenny had been back there. Captain Wainwright said that she had, but only to find out if he knew where the Monroes lived. He did not know, and so she left again. He had offered to let her stay on the ship, but she had seemed worried and did not think that was a good idea.

John spent a miserable night, not knowing how he was going to find her again, and not knowing how she would have fared through the night. The only place she knew to meet him was at *Reynold's Inn*, and she was probably afraid to go back there because of Hanson.

He was sitting at breakfast with his father and mother,

and they spent much time talking back and forth and discussing various ideas for finding Jenny. They finally decided that she had a far better chance of finding them than they had of finding her. All she needed to do was make discrete inquires around town until she found someone who knew where the Monroes lived. That being settled, they sat for a time in silence, and afterwards John mentioned dully that he had heard Mr. Whitefield preach out at sea.

"Did you?" his mother said, excited.

"Mr. Whitefield is a good man," his father said. "I heard yesterday that he is going to be preaching between here and Baltimore today. Most of the shops here will be closed. The streets will be deserted. But I hope the people listen and not just go for the spectacle."

"I know you say Mr. Whitefield is a good man," John said, "and I have heard you say it before. But you say it as though he might not be, or that something might be wrong. Is that what you mean?"

His father waited a few minutes before answering. "I am in two minds about what he is doing, John. When I go to St. Anne's and hear our dear vicar preach, I am prepared for him to disappear at any time in a cloud of dust, leaving nothing behind but a few vestments. And men like him have pursued Mr. Whitefield out of the church, hounding him in an awful way. And all because God uses Mr. Whitefield to preach life into bones. And there are many bones to be preached to, believe you me, and I don't mean in the churchyard."

John sat quietly, very gratified that his father was speaking to him about this so openly. Before this, he had only been able to go on the basis of bits and pieces. "So what concerns you about Mr. Whitefield then?"

"I have read some of the accounts of the revivals, particularly those in New England, and some of the enthusiasts seem to have far too much free rein. Mr. Edwards is a decent and sober man, but Mr. Davenport most emphatically is not. Playing with wildfire will sometimes keep you warm, but other times the destruction can be great."

John sat and waited for his father to continue. "The shepherds have chased a true shepherd out of the folds, and he is preaching to the sheep in the fields. But this is a new country, John, and look to the west. The fields are much larger than the folds. I am not sure that we will ever be able to get the sheep back into the folds again."

John nodded, and just listened. "Go back to fire. Our vicar has a lovely fireplace, and nothing in it but ashes. And our open-air preachers have the fire—they certainly have the fire. But they don't have the fireplace, and I think we need both. But all the same, I think we should go hear Mr. Whitefield if we can."

Jane Monroe suddenly stood to her feet and pointed out the window. "Is that Jenny?"

John leaned over the table and looked out. Jenny was

standing hesitantly at the front gate, trying to decide whether to open it. John jumped to his feet, and rushed to the front door. "Yes!"

There was a great bustle as she was escorted into the house. John introduced her to his parents, and Jenny curtsied clumsily because she was still holding her very important package. "Thank you, ma'am," she said when Jane Monroe offered her some food. "I haven't eaten since yesterday."

"I am very sorry," John said. "What happened?"

Jenny explained to them the encounter with Hanson at *Reynold's Inn,* and it was very much like what John had imagined. But the two villains had done the same thing to Jenny that they had done to John in the elm tree—although Jenny did not have an elm tree in which to hide. She had seen them coming up the street and had no time to move or hide. But they did not look at her and had walked deliberately up the stairs. Then they had stopped at the door and talked for a few minutes about whether they wanted to go inside and ask about John and Jenny—although they did not know John's name. She just sat silently on the bench looking down, hoping and praying that they would not look over at her. As soon as they decided to go in, she waited until the door clicked shut, grabbed her package and rushed off past the church. "I was very lucky they didn't see me," she said.

"I don't believe in luck," Thomas Monroe said. "But you were blessed."

Jenny sat down at the Monroe table humbly, her package on her lap. John's mother had the cook bring out some breakfast for her. Jenny thanked the cook gratefully, pushed her raven hair gracefully behind her ears and bowed her head to say grace. Jane Monroe decided with satisfaction that she liked this girl very much. She was pious, polite, beautiful and reminded Jane of a favorite aunt. John found out many years later that all his good fortune dated from that moment.

"Did you sleep?" Thomas Monroe asked anxiously. Jenny nodded, her mouth full. A moment later she said, "I found an inn close to the river. It was not bad."

"After you eat," Mrs. Monroe said, "we have some dresses here that I think will fit you."

"Thank you very much, ma'am" Jenny said. "I am very sorry to have come here like this . . . I am so sorry to be so much trouble. And I have caused John so much trouble and danger . . . ," but Jane Monroe shushed her.

"Have you heard that Mr. Whitefield is going to be preaching near here?" John asked her.

Jenny looked up, her brown eyes wide. "Is he? Are you going to hear him?"

Thomas Monroe stood up. "I'll have the stable hands prepare the coach. We should leave within an hour or so. Can you all be ready?"

When Jenny had breakfasted, John's mother escorted her off to her room, and John was pleased to hear them chatting

pleasantly up the stairs. The coach was ready out in front of
the house in about forty-five minutes, with a driver and footman standing patiently by. Jenny came down the stairs shortly
after, followed by John's mother, and both John and Thomas
were much astonished at the transformation in her. She had
not had time to do much besides change her dress and ar-
range her hair, but John suddenly realized that her old clothes
really had been rags.

The four of them stood by the front door for a moment,
when Jenny, who was feeling wonderful, decided to tease
John a little bit. "The only problem with going to hear Mr.
Whitefield is that, afterwards, we shall have to keep John out
of fights."

"What? What is that?" said both parents, and the door
closed behind them.

As they approached the field where Mr. Whitefield was
scheduled to preach, John looked out the window and saw
dust ascending everywhere. Not only from the road their
coach was on, but also from a number of other roads converg-
ing at the turnpike. There was a great open field off to the left
of the road, with an ascending slope at one end, and people

were streaming into it from every direction. There were thousands of people. Farmers were trotting alongside horses with two or three children riding. Men and women were walking together. Coaches were crowded together with farm wagons. Mules, horses and donkeys were tied off on countless bushes and trees.

A small platform had been built on the ascending slope of the field, and there was a small cluster of clergymen assembled there. John recognized several of them as Presbyterian parsons with their clerical tabs, and Mr. Whitefield was standing in the center. Another man was there in farmer's clothing, and John thought he might be the Baptist minister. Rumor had it that he was conducting meetings in homes, and a number of people had been greatly scandalized by it. But he seemed to be on good terms with the other ministers here. They all appeared to be praying together.

"Isn't that wonderful?" he said to his father, pointing to them.

"Yes," his father said, nodding. "but not nearly wonderful enough. And very dangerous. Just like the gospel—very dangerous." John thought his father was speaking in riddles again, and decided to ask him about what he meant later. They had left the coachman and footman with the coach. "They will certainly be able to hear," said John's father. "And I picked the two most likely to benefit from this experience. They probably know it, too."

The four of them were able to pick their way to a place near the platform. John looked back around him and noted that the field was very nearly full. There were tens of thousands of people here. *How could they all hear?* John wondered. But he need not have wondered. Mr. Whitefield's voice had carried wonderfully at sea, but he did almost as well here. He opened with prayer and announced his text, which was from Jeremiah—"The Lord Our Righteousness." He began to preach and a heavy silence fell upon the crowd.

Whoever is acquainted with the nature of mankind in general, or the propensity of his own heart in particular, must acknowledge, that self-righteousness is the last idol that is rooted out of the heart . . .

John had heard Mr. Whitefield preach before, but this time he was confronted not only with the preaching, but with the dramatic effects of the preaching all around him. In just a few minutes, he could hear a few people quietly sobbing, but there were no hysterics. He stood there silently, together with Jenny, and with his father and mother, meditating on the words of the sermon.

Indeed, our Lord does recommend morality and good works, (as all faithful ministers will do), and clears the moral law from many corrupt glosses put upon it by the letter-learned Pharisees . . .

John was looking absently over Mr. Whitefield's head—he found some of his gestures distracting—and he suddenly stiffened. There in a tree, right behind Mr. Whitefield's head was Hanson, carefully scanning the crowd.

Susan Creek

JOHN TOOK JENNY BY THE ELBOW, AND PULLED
her slowly to stand behind Thomas Monroe. John had
been wearing a tri-corner hat which he had taken off during
the prayer, and he now put it back on and pulled it down over
his eyes. There was no need for his parents to do anything
because what they looked like was not known to Hanson and
his confederate at all. He then leaned over and whispered to
his father that Hanson was up in the tree. There were others
up in trees listening to Mr. Whitefield also, so it took a moment for John to explain which one was Hanson. But once he
was identified, it was hard to miss him. He spent all his time
looking over the crowd with a hostile glare, as unregenerate
as you please.

The four stood quietly until it appeared that Mr. Whitefield was approaching the conclusion of his message, and so they began working their way back to the coach, but slowly, so as to not attract attention to their movement. Others were moving toward the edge of the crowd also, but not many. As they made their way out, John kept checking to see if Hanson was still there—which he was, except for the last glance. When they were right at the edge of the crowd, he looked back one more time, and the tree was empty. Maybe he had seen them getting away, or maybe he just wanted to move out to the road in order to look at the part of the crowd that was moving back toward Annapolis. John didn't know, but he caught up with his father and told him that Hanson was down from the tree.

Thomas urged them all to pick up their pace, and in just a few more minutes they were back at the coach. They all clambered in, and Mr. Monroe told the coachman to take them out at a moderate trot. John, looking back again, saw a man that looked like Hanson emerge from the crowd and take a station next to a tree where he could watch everyone stream by. He must not have seen them, and they made it safely away.

Their conversation on the way back to town was scattered. Some of it had to do with the sermon, some with the men who were looking for them, and some of the conversation concerned both topics together. "How could a man like that climb a tree right behind Mr. Whitefield's head," Jenny asked, "and not repent and believe?"

"That's because he had other things on his mind," John said. "He was busy thinking about cutting our throats."

"John!" Jane Monroe stared at her son.

When they arrived back in Annapolis, Thomas decided they needed a plan of action. The four of them all sat around the table, and Jenny had gone upstairs and brought down her bundle of papers. "I understand some of this," she said. "But you will have to help me with it. I don't think my mother understood all of it, either—just enough so that we knew we had to run."

She opened the bundle and pushed it across the table to Thomas Monroe. "What is King George's War?" she asked.

"There was trouble with succession to the Austrian throne after the death of the Emperor Charles in '40," Thomas said.

"Oh, I know about that," Jenny said.

"Well, whenever war breaks out in Europe, of course it affects all of us here. The French have stirred up some of the Indians against us again, and we call it King George's War here. They call it something else in the Old World. But most of the fighting over here has been in Nova Scotia and New York. The French and their tribes burned Saratoga last year after the Iroquois joined with us against them. But in the New World, it is not a war really—more like periodic raids. But it has happened mostly in the north, and the tribes down here in the middle colonies have been very quiet."

"Well, that's what this is about then," said Jenny. "Look at that paper—yes, that one there."

Thomas stared at the paper, his brow furrowing. He read quietly for some time and then read through some other papers that Jenny gave him. He was obviously getting more from it than Jenny or her mother had done. When he was done, he put them all down, and the others looked at him anxiously. "What is it?" Jane asked him.

"Major Hanson is in the pay of the French crown. There is a letter here from him to the Marquis Delacroix, in which he identifies three English spies in the French forces. According to Hanson, those spies are the reason why the French have been unable to stir up the tribes through the middle colonies. Every offer they make is somehow mysteriously countered by the English, and the tribes down here have stayed neutral. But if they went on the warpath, it would cause great consternation in London, and they might even negotiate away vast tracts of land in the interior. Some courtiers are even urging that the king give up the Ohio valley *now* for the sake of peace with France."

"Where is the marquis?" John asked.

"At a place west of here called Susan Creek. He is a fur trader—doesn't look like a marquis at all. But he is a French nobleman, and his purpose there is to maintain communication with the French forces. He is apparently the one who gets all the messages to and from the French crown. All concealed in bundles of beaver pelts, I'll warrant."

They all sat around the table in silence.

Then John said, "Was Hanson planning to come over here himself? It seems to me that he wrote the letter because he wasn't. Maybe he came over because Jenny had the letter. Originally, he must have meant to send the letter by courier. Is that right?"

"That seems to make sense." Thomas nodded.

"And the marquis wouldn't necessarily know what that courier looked like."

Thomas scratched the back of his neck thoughtfully. "I think I see your meaning. Perhaps someone else might show up at Susan Creek? Give him some of these papers, but not all of them? Give him a few forgeries mixed in? How about a plan of the English to march on Quebec? We could keep some of the French forces up north marching around busily."

Jane was sitting quietly, hands in her lap. "I am not sure that I wanted this. I worried far more than I should have when John was out at sea. It is my besetting ... But duty comes to us all."

"What name does the marquis go by?" Jenny asked

Thomas answered, "His own—Jacques Delacroix. He has simply dropped the marquis. It is all right here."

After much discussion, it was decided that John would go with Thomas to Susan Creek. They would be Thomas and John Morton from Charleston, and they would tell Jacques that Mr. Hanson sends his regards. They would not understand much, but they did know that it was important for this particular packet to come into Mr. Delacroix's hands. John looked over at his father and saw that in spite of the serious front he was putting up for his mother's sake, he was thoroughly enjoying himself. And John felt exactly the same way.

Thomas Monroe spent the evening trying to match Major Hanson's signature for the letter that he would forge concerning the impending march on Quebec.

In the morning, John came down from his bedroom and looked out the front window. There, in the semi-circled lane in front of the house, stood a stable hand with the reins of two saddled and prepared horses in his hands. The sun was out, and it was to be a glorious day. But even though it was spring, John could see the breath of the horses rising as they champed and stomped impatiently.

His father was at the table, eating his breakfast hurriedly. His mouth full, he gestured to John to do the same, and John fell to with a will. John's mother and Jenny were in the backroom, visiting as though they were mother and daughter, and after a few minutes they came out to see their men off. "You be careful, Thomas Monroe," said Jane. "Trust in the Lord, honor the king, and do what is right."

"Yes, ma'am" said Thomas, and kissed his wife affection-
ately. "Don't start fretting," Thomas said to her. "I will try," she
said. John kissed his mother, said good bye to Jenny, and out the
door they went.

Thomas knew the way to the Susan Creek outpost and
thought that they would be about four hours getting there.
"Although I have only been out there twice before. I can't be
sure." The sun by this point was over the trees, and the day
was warming up nicely. The ride was extremely pleasant, and
John alternated between looking forward to their excitement
and simply enjoying being back in Maryland. The time went
by swiftly as John and his father caught up on all that had happened since John last put to sea. The road was in good shape,
and the budding green trees covered the hills gently. John was
as contented as he had ever been, and he didn't know why—
since they were off to trick a spy, contentment did not seem like
the appropriate response.

At last they came to the ridge of a hill, overlooking a small
but beautiful valley. Thomas pointed to the right—"Susan
Creek runs down that slope, and down through the ravine. I
don't know why they call it a creek—it's a brook really. Not at
all like the creeks back off the Severn. But the brook runs down
through a cluster of buildings right near where it joins the river—there. The largest building—see it?—is where I fancy we
shall find Mr. Delacroix." The two nudged their horses into a
canter, and they made their way down the sloping road.

When they arrived, they tied off their horses in the front of the large clapboard warehouse, and stepped carefully inside. Off to the left were stacks of pelts and furs, and to the right was the jumbled contents of a general store. There was a small office back of the counter, and it was lit much more effectively than the rest of the store. A small, energetic-looking man was in the office. He jumped up when he heard them shut the door, and came out to greet them. Thomas removed his tri-corner, as did John, and greeted the proprietor. "Mr. Delacroix?"

"Yes?"

"Mr. Hanson sends his regards. I am Thomas Morton of Charleston, and this is my son, John. I have something that I am to deliver to you. Mr. Hanson said that you must give it your most urgent attention." Thomas handed over the packet, and received a small, heavy bag in exchange. He and John stepped back on the other side of the counter as Mr. Delacroix opened the package, and read through it hurriedly.

The effect was far, far beyond their expectations. Mr. Delacroix suddenly stood up stiff with an exclamation, and began to throw some things together. He came out of his small office. "You will excuse me, monsieurs? I am much in your debt." With that, he dashed out a back door. A few moments later the father and son heard the sound of galloping hooves. "Off to Quebec," Thomas said.

John stepped outside with his father, looked across at him and said, "Well, that was easy."

The Seat of Scoffers

THE FATHER AND SON DID NOT FEEL LIKE climbing back on their horses for the long ride home, and John was somewhat let down by his first foray into espionage. The Frenchman had believed them, just like that, and galloped off to the north. Now they had a four-hour ride home, and *then* they would get to tell their adventures to the ladies. "And *then* he got on his horse, and rode off!" John was more than a little annoyed, and though his father did not say anything, John suspected the same was true for him.

So they walked down to the river and threw a few rocks into it. For the first time in his life, John outthrew his father, and the pleasure that *that* gave him lifted the annoyance somewhat. After distance throwing, target throwing and skipping rocks,

Thomas finally said, "Let's go back up to the town, what there is of it and see if there is any place that serves victuals. We can eat, and then, back to Annapolis."

John nodded glumly. They made their way back up to the cluster of buildings, and went from one building to another, looking for one that might be a tavern. "When trappers come in from the mountains," Thomas said, "they are always thirsty and usually hungry. There has to be something here somewhere."

As luck played out, they found it in the last building they checked. The front door was around the back and faced the woods in an odd, rebellious kind of way. A ramshackle porch slanted precariously toward the ground in front of the porch. When they came around from the road and looked at it, they could see the first real signs of human activity since they had arrived—not counting Mr. Delacroix's alacrity. The door was shutting behind a man who was just going in.

They followed him and stepped into the tavern but had considerable difficulty making anything out at first. It was very dark, and smoke filled the upper half of the room. They could see a few scattered frontiersmen sitting around at various tables and a very large, greasy man standing behind what seemed to be some kind of a counter.

They walked up to him, and he greeted them in a fashion that in any other setting would have been described as surly, but here, it seemed positively cordial. "What'll ye have?"

"Two pints of ale," said Thomas. "And what do you have to eat?"

"Stew," he said. "Bear stew."

"Two bowls of that, then," Thomas said.

Thomas and John gathered their rough dinner and made their way to a back table. Thomas motioned to John that they should both sit with their backs to the wall. John raised his eyebrows, somewhat puzzled, but took his place on the rough cut wooden bench that ran along the wall.

"We don't get many *gentlemen* in these parts," came a voice from their left. "Judging from the cut of your clothes, you *are* gentlemen, aren't you?"

"I am Thomas Morton of Charleston," Thomas said. "This is my son, John. I suppose some would consider us gentlemen."

"I ain't never had any truck with any gentlemen nohow," the voice came back.

"We had no intention of violating any of your local customs," Thomas replied cordially. "And we will be on our way just as soon as we finish our stew." And with that, he took out a pistol from within his coat, and laid it on the table with a genial smile. This startled John somewhat, but he did the same a second later. He had brought with him the brace of pistols that James Gunn had given him back in Scotland, but he only took one of them out. *Two pistols would be far too much,* he thought. *We don't want to be provocative.*

This action silenced the belligerent ruffian, whoever he was, but the tension in the room was ramped up considerably.

Everyone there had noticed the exchange, and everything was very quiet. Thomas and John continued to eat, and everyone there just sat in silence. John had looked around the room carefully and seen only three figures sitting in the gloom, not counting the cook behind the counter. He and his father each had a cutlass, John had two pistols (both loaded), and Thomas had one. John was not sure why, but the annoyance he had felt earlier was completely gone. He glanced over at his father, and thought that he was feeling the same way. He leaned over and whispered, "Are you enjoying yourself?"

His father pursed his lips, tapped on his bowl with his spoon, and thought for a moment. "Yes, I am." he finally said. "But don't tell your mother."

John laughed and returned to his stew, which was almost gone. Just when he was scraping the last portions of it into his spoon—it was surprisingly good—he heard the door creak open again, and looked up. His eyes had adjusted to the inside of the tavern completely, and so he had no difficulty recognizing Major Hanson and his murderous companion. I wonder what his name is? John thought. In spite of himself, he had jumped in his seat, and then immediately hoped his father hadn't noticed. He leaned over and whispered to his father—"that's Hanson!"

Hanson walked deliberately up to the cook, and asked, "Where is Delacroix?"

The cook stood puzzled, wiping his hands on his apron. "He ran over here about an hour and a half ago. Said he had a message from you, and he had to leave for Quebec immediately. He asked us to mind the warehouse while he was gone."

Hanson swore savagely and turned around. When he did, his eyes came to rest on Thomas and John, and he stood bolt upright. Thomas waved at him jovially. Hanson pointed at the two of them and began fumbling for his sword. His companion had his sword out first and lunged toward their table. Thomas picked up his pistol and coolly shot him through the heart, toppling him like a tree. John had his pistol leveled at Hanson, but was immediately distracted by a figure coming at them from the left. It was their earlier disputant, the one who now had a reason to fight the gentlemen.

John swerved in his seat and fired his pistol at the darkest part of the looming shadow. He heard a gasp of pain, and a body fell by their feet. He was a man in buckskin, a man with an enormous beard. John heard the sound of a death rattle, but by this time he was on his feet and had his sword out. Thomas had done the same on the other side of the table, and the two began to make their way to the door. The others in the inn kept their seats as Hanson dashed for the door. John fumbled for his other pistol, but by the time he had it out, Hanson had completely disappeared.

The two followed him out the door and were standing outside trying to decide which way he had gone, when the door opened again, and the others, cook and all, streamed out. They were all armed and had apparently taken up the cause of the fleeing Hanson. "Come this way, John," Thomas said, and the two ran around the corner of the building, back to where their horses were tied. But the others knew the layout of their small village much better than Thomas did, and when the two came into the street, between them and their horses were three armed but stationary men, and all of them angry.

Thomas leaned over to John and said, "After you shoot one of them, we will have a fair swordfight, one on one. The cook has the longest arms and might be the biggest trouble when we close to fight. So I suggest you shoot him. But wait until we are about ten yards apart. After that distance, the ball from one of those pistols starts to float every which way, just like a butterfly. If you hit anything after that point, it is only because of the sovereignty of God."

John nodded, and slowly the two of them began to walk toward the three men who were blocking their path. As they closed upon them, John felt an eagerness for the fight descend upon him. *This what they call Mars,* he thought. Inside the tavern, he and his father had fought because they had to, in the suddenness of the moment. But here they were advancing because they wanted to, and John wondered briefly how many sons had gone into battle at their father's right hand.

"Now," said his father. "Fire."

John raised his pistol, which the three men had apparently not seen and were not ready for. His hand came up in a fluid motion, and John felt the gun go off in his hand. As he watched the cook go over backwards, clutching at his chest, John suddenly thought of Curtis. *He had killed two men today, but this was nothing like the fight with Curtis.* His conscience had bothered him before, during and after the fight with Curtis, and it had just been a fist fight. Now he was in a fight in which he was killing men, and he was nothing but grateful to be fighting alongside his father, a good and godly man.

The two remaining men looked at the cook on the ground with consternation, and then turned back to face Thomas and John, who were still advancing with their swords up. But the fight had gone out of them, and after they parried some initial thrusts for just a few moments, they turned tail and ran. Thomas turned back and stooped over the cook. "He's dead," he said, standing up. "I suggest we ride."

John untied his horse, and settled him down, patting his neck for a few moments—the gunshot had startled him greatly. Thomas was doing this same with his horse, and after they were calmed, the father and son swung into their saddles. They trotted to the edge of the village and up the path toward the main road.

"This is probably the way that Hanson went," Thomas said. "I suggest that you reload."

John had left one pistol back in the tavern, but when his father spoke, he already had the other one out again and was pouring powder down the barrel.

Hanson the Fugitive

WHY DIDN'T YOU SHOOT HANSON IN THE LEG?"
Thomas asked. "Then we would have some blood on
the path to follow."

John laughed. "Because then the other would have killed us,
and we wouldn't be following anyone except for all our ances-
tors. And besides, I thought you knew how to track."

"I know how to hunt with dogs," Thomas said glumly.
"When I try to track by looking at the ground, all I see is dirt.
Which is why it would be nice if Hanson were bleeding on the
path here. You are a very disobedient son for failing to antici-
pate my desires in this."

"What we need to do," said John, ignoring his father, "is
make good time back to Annapolis. That is where he is no

doubt going. If it is, we can try to deal with him if he tries to do anything there. And if he isn't going there, then we don't care, do we?"

"Hanson appears to be a dangerous scoundrel. We need to exhibit the right kind of public spirit, Jonathan. We must try to remove him from our public affairs."

At the top of the slope that ran down to Susan Creek the two slowed their horses to a walk. And it was there that John began to realize the enormity of the fight they had just been in. He looked down at his hand, the one that had fired both shots, and wondered why it wasn't shaking.

"Have you ever killed anyone, father?"

Thomas shook his head. "No. That was the first time."

"What are we supposed to feel?"

His father took a moment, but John could see that he was composing a reply carefully. "Though I have never killed a man, I have been in a few situations where I thought I was going to have to. Afterwards, I studied the Scriptures thoroughly. I was more frightened that I had almost killed someone without knowing what the Bible said than by anything else. One of your mother's cousins is a Quaker, and when I came back from that incident she had challenged me to consider the ways of Jesus. Of course, as Christians, this is something that we all must do, and I had not done it. And so I accepted what she said, at least as far as considering it. But after my study, I decided it is very easy to impose upon Jesus things He never said or thought."

"Like thinking that Jesus would never kill a man?"

"Yes. He would not do that during His time on earth because that was not His mission. He came to seek and to save that which was lost. But the Bible also says that when He returns, it will not be the same story. The slain shall fill his path."

"So sometimes we must kill, and sometimes not?"

"That is what Ecclesiastes says: 'A time for war, a time for peace.'"

"But the men we killed have eternal souls. And because of what we did, they went to meet God. And I just read yesterday that when the wicked man dies, his hope perishes. And we had to decide in just seconds what we were supposed to do. Then, they were dead."

"That is why you must do your thinking beforehand. That is why your mother and I had to bring you up in the nurture and admonition of the Lord. When Hanson came in the tavern, you could not hold up your hand and ask everyone to wait while you searched the Scriptures."

John laughed again. "Yes, and if good men do not kill bad men, then bad men will kill good men. Which means that at the bottom, good men who refuse to fight are killing other good men."

"You have understood it well. We are created in Christ Jesus to do good works, which God prepared beforehand for us to do.

When the circumstances are right, killing the wicked is a portion of the good works that God has prepared for us to do. But like everything else, we are to do what we do in faith and not rely on our own wisdom. And remember, Jesus not only kills men—He kills every man, including the men who died today."

"Your cousin the Quaker was not persuaded by this?"

"Not even close," Thomas laughed. "She left our home in a thorough-going huff. We have never seen her since. You should have seen her flounce her skirts before she got in her carriage."

The two spent the next several hours talking about this and other related things. Thomas had always taught John carefully when he was small, but John felt for the first time that he was learning from his father as a man. Maybe it was because he had fought alongside his father and had killed two men. But John did not really think that was it.

They had been making good time along the main road. They crested a ridge, from which the road descended in a straight line and then ran up an opposing hill. Several miles away, they could make out a lone horseman, almost to the top of that hill.

"Is that Hanson?" John asked.

"Let's find out," his father said, spurring his horse to a full gallop. John did the same a second later, and within a few moments they were both flying down the hill, full tilt. For a short time, there was no change in the distant horseman's behavior, but he looked over his shoulder soon enough. When he did so, Hanson—for it *was* Hanson—spurred his horse and galloped up over the ridge. As soon as he disappeared from sight, Thomas pulled his horse up and stopped.

"We will not catch him this way, but at least we can make his ride back to Annapolis a little more exciting for him."

They both slowed their horses to a walk, and resumed their conversation. "You should notice something else about this, John. Have you done so?"

"Clearly not," said John.

"This is the way that many battles go and many wars as well. When you came back to our home, Hanson was pursuing you. Now we are pursuing him. Whenever you are attacked, it is never enough simply to stand your ground. You must turn to the offensive, you must always look to attack."

"I think I understand," John said.

"When we were in the road, and they were standing between us and our horses, it was very important for us to advance toward them. If we had backed away, the chances are very good that the story would have ended unhappily for your mother."

"And Jenny," said John.

"Ah, yes, Jenny," Thomas said, looking at his son sideways. "She seems a very nice girl."

"Yes, she is," John said. "Despite her circumstances."

Thomas just waited after this last comment because it

seemed obvious to him that John wanted to talk. And talk he did, pouring out to his father the whole story of how Jenny and her mother came into possession of the papers in the first place, how she responded to Mr. Whitefield's preaching, and how she wanted to go to a church where the ministers didn't creak when they walked.

"Well, that's not our church," Thomas said, rubbing his chin. "Maybe your mother and I need to have another conversation. You and Jenny may want to go to the stables for church this next Lord's Day. Maybe we will follow."

"Now that I am back from sea," John said, "what do you want me to do?"

"Your mother and I enjoy living in the town house very much. But we need someone to take up residence in the creek house, south of Annapolis. You remember staying there when you were a small boy?"

John nodded eagerly. One of his favorite memories had been that of sliding down the steep slopes covered with leaves and acorns, sliding joyfully down toward the creek. He must have been four years old, and he remembered the contentment of that afternoon as though it had been yesterday afternoon. Thomas decided that now was the time to bring John into the family secret and hand over to him the responsibility of guarding it.

"You know that your grandmother was a woman named Sarah Ingle. She had a son by her first marriage, a worthy young man named Thomas. In the course of his adventures, he found a pirate treasure in a cave on that property. Like the shrewd young man he was, he enlisted the help of John Monroe, your grandfather, in buying that property. Captain Monroe married your grandmother, and they used the treasure sparingly and wisely to establish our business in Annapolis. But most of it is still there."

"Still there?" James gasped.

"Still there. But someone needs to live there and manage the two plantations we have to the west of that place. Old Williams has gotten too old to manage it all successfully. I want to set him up in a small cabin out there, where he can finish his days fishing in the creek. If you can find him, you can ask him questions about how to manage the place. Are you willing?"

"Willing? I love that place. You would trust me with it?"

"I will, if you remember two things. First, Williams is an old black man who is wiser than you will ever be. Ask him as many questions as you can without pestering him in his old age. And second, do you think Jenny would be willing to live there?"

"Jenny?" John flushed a deep red. "Do you think I am ready to marry?"

"Well, no, of course not. No man is ever ready. That's why God makes us do it."

John felt briefly annoyed on top of his embarrassment. "That doesn't make any sense to me, Father. How can a man know that he is ready for something by knowing that he is not ready? How can he distinguish himself from the man who really is not ready?"

His father grinned broadly. "It is very simple, really. The ones who know they are not ready are ready. The ones who know they are ready are not. And besides, you need someone to help you with that annoyance problem of yours. The world does not need any more Christians who furrow their brow so easily. And judging from the results thus far, the next person attempting this work with you needs to be much prettier than I."

In spite of himself, John grimaced, then laughed and then grimaced again.

The Royal Governor

WHEN THEY ARRIVED BACK IN ANNAPOLIS, the women were overjoyed to see them, and as they sat around, well into the evening, they had to tell the story over and over again. Jenny was particularly delighted with how Mr. Delacroix had headed north to warn the French immediately. But when they were finally done talking about the day's events, Thomas Monroe changed the subject.

"Well, tomorrow I suppose we shall have to go see the governor."

"Why?" John asked.

"There is a spy for the French in his town, and someone has just left the colony to warn the French in the north about a non-existent invasion. I think we need to tell the governor."

"Why didn't we tell him before?" Jenny asked innocently.

Thomas coughed politely. "I hate to be disrespectful of the established authorities. But the royal governor is a preeminently useless individual. If I had told him about this when something needed to be done, it would most certainly not have been done. Afterwards, we can give him information about it so that he can feel important as he drafts letters to London. That way, he will not be angry with us. We have spared him the agony of making decisions, and we can give him leave to take as much of the credit as he pleases. Which, no doubt, will be considerable."

"Is this Governor Bradstreet?" John asked.

"No, he was a good man. He left for England only about a month after you sailed the last time, John. Governor Simon has only been here for a few months, but that has been more than enough time to take the measure of the man. His inaugural address to the legislature was a sight to behold."

"What did he do?" Jenny asked.

"He paraded in with his fawning courtiers—as though he were a prince and not a colonial governor—and had two concubines with him. He then spoke to us all with such an effeminate lisp that we began to be glad for the presence of the concubines..."

"Thomas!" said Jane.

"And I have never heard such a patronizing speech in my life. We were the colonial inhabitants of this backwater province, and he had arrived to bring us light and life and glory and civilization. He would raise us to the level of London society. But from what I have heard of London society, reaching that level could not precisely be described as a *raising*. The difference between English morals and ours will not come to a good end, I tell you. He has not had a moment's cooperation from the legislature since, and, of course, he believes it to be because we are obtuse. But we still need to go talk to him, if only just to observe the formalities."

And so it was that the next morning, Thomas Monroe sent a slave over to the governor's mansion with a card, asking for an appointment. One was quickly granted, and the slave returned within the half hour, saying that the governor would receive them after luncheon.

"You all go," Jane said. "I have just been observing this adventure and have not really played a role in it. I do not really need to go, and, Lord forgive me, I cannot abide the man."

Thomas nodded, and so the rest of them spent the morning discussing what they would tell the governor. After they had eaten, they put on their best clothes—Mrs. Monroe helped Jenny out again—and because it was a beautiful day, they all walked the few blocks over to the governor's residence. They pulled the bell rope at the front door, and after a few moments, a black servant appeared. He bowed as though he was expecting them and stepped aside to usher them in the door.

The entryway was paneled with a rich walnut, and the floor was the same. Around the walls were rows upon rows of muskets—the hallway of the governor was the arsenal of the town. It really created a grand effect. An oriental carpet covered most of the floor, and the three spoke softly with one another as the servant took their coats and Jenny's wrap. After a moment the servant reappeared and said, "This way, please."

They followed him to the mansion's library and filed into that room after the servant stood to the side. The servant reached in and pulled the door shut behind them. Across the room, reclining in a chair by the cold spring fireplace, they saw what could only be the royal governor. Right next to him, in his full dress uniform, was Major Hanson—smiling grimly and with what appeared to be deep satisfaction. The governor was slouched in his chair, complaining under his breath about something.

John and Jenny looked at Thomas Monroe, who (unlike them) had taken this new development completely in stride. Thomas walked deliberately toward the governor, bowed and introduced himself. They had met several times before, but after their first meeting Thomas was convinced that the governor was not capable of remembering anything of value. And it obviously would not do for him to be Thomas Morton of Charleston here—he was known to everyone in town *except* for Major Hanson. And so it was time for Hanson to learn his real name. And the governor, suddenly remembering himself, also introduced Major Hanson to them—as his new adjutant.

During these moments, Thomas was thinking quickly about what they could report. They had earlier decided to tell the governor that there was an English army officer named Hanson in the colony, out of uniform, working for the French. But since they had given most of the papers to Delacroix, they had nothing with which to prove this charge. But if Hanson had not been there, they might not have had to prove it. They could have simply informed the governor about what they had heard, and that he should be attentive. They could have then departed, having done their duty. But now, it would not do to simply announce without proof that Major Hanson was a spy. And yet, because Hanson was here with the governor, this must mean that he had received orders to come to America and was here under some sort of false mission. This also probably meant that his superiors in Scotland were part of this plot with the French. And how had they arranged for him to be the governor's adjutant?

And so Thomas decided that audacity was the only hope. He needed to lie, and to do so in such a way that Hanson would recognize the lie, but not be able to contradict it. And that meant it had to have a large measure of truth in it. And Hanson had to be placed in a position where he must work against himself.

"Governor Simon," Thomas began. "I am sorry to trouble you with something like this so early in your tenure with us. But I am afraid we have a traitor in our midst, someone who is working with the French against the crown's interest in the

lands west of the mountains. Just yesterday I received a letter from a friend in Parliament, and he informs me that an
English officer has turned coat, and has fled to take refuge in
the colonies. He is accompanied by a young woman—about
the age of this young lady—and they have information that
would be extremely damaging to us in our cause against the
French papists. You will receive a packet from the king's sec-
retary confirming all this within just a few weeks. And I have
friends to the west who have informed me that a French merchant there named Jacques Delacroix has fled the colony. He
must have received information that you had learned who his
informant was to be. We do not know any of their names, but
we know their description. If I may make a suggestion, I would
ask that you assign a contingent of soldiers to watch the harbor for the next several weeks. Check all passengers as they
disembark? Perhaps you could assign—is it Major Hanson?—
to head their efforts."

In response, Hanson just glared at Thomas Monroe, filled
with animosity. The governor did not notice any of this, being
the kind of man who noticed only himself. But by this time,
Hanson knew that Thomas could not prove anything against
him. For if he could, why tell this cock and bull story? But neither
could Hanson prove anything against Thomas Monroe, who
was obviously a respected man in the community. Everything
was now a manner of settling scores privately, a task which
Hanson had clearly resolved to do.

The governor waved his lace handkerchief wearily. "That is good. Hanson, assemble some soldiers to do just that, and report back to me when you have done so." Hanson indulged in one last glare before leaving the room, and the three were then left alone with the governor.

"One last thing, governor" said Thomas, stepping forward and lowering his voice. "I did not want to say anything when your adjutant was here—not that I suspect him, of course—but one of the things that my friend warned me about was that this English officer, whoever he is, was also assigned to assassinate you. If you want my advice, I would require that all your officers fulfill all their duties from this point only in pairs. Leave none of them alone for a moment, and that way they will never be free to consider harming you in any way."

The governor was the kind of man who did not require proof if anything threatened his person in any fashion, and so he believed Thomas's story completely. Jenny said afterwards that she had never seen anyone believe anything so completely. "Not even at Mr. Whitefield's meeting," she said. "That's what comes from being a freethinker," Thomas Monroe had replied. "Unbelievers will believe anything."

By now Governor Simon's eyes were wide and filled with fear and concern. His hands were both trembling, and he assured Thomas Monroe that he would do exactly that. And he asked Mr. Monroe if he would look in on him daily, to see if he was well. Picking up a bell on a table next to him, he rang it vigorously. A servant appeared, and the governor ordered an-other officer, a man named Miller, to appear before him. He would give the order for all officers, as long as they were in uniform and on duty, to double up right away. They, in their turn, would take this as merely another eccentricity from an already eccentric governor. Except perhaps for Major Hanson, but there was nothing he could do about it.

As Thomas Monroe prepared for the three of them to take their leave, the governor effused over them with gratitude. "I am so very grateful for your kindness," he said. "If I can ever repay you, please inform me of it at once."

Thomas Monroe bowed once again. "I am at your service," he said.

Battle on Prince George's Avenue

SEVERAL WEEKS WENT BY. JOHN SAW MAJOR Hanson two times during that period, and both times he was in the company of another officer. John smiled at him, knowing that if Hanson had been alone, John would have had to watch his back and stay away from alleys.

After the second time, he asked his father that evening what they could do. Hanson was here in Annapolis as the governor's adjutant, and, even though Delacroix was gone for the time being, he would be back at some point. And they could not leave Hanson alone to scheme through a way to avenge himself. "We have to do something," John said. "We have to get Hanson out of the colony. After that, we can tell the governor the whole story."

"I know," Thomas said. "And the governor is starting to ask me about the packet I said was coming from London. My little story bought us some time, but not enough, I fear."

"Why did Hanson become a traitor?" Jane Monroe suddenly asked, turning to Jenny.

"It was not through any noble principle," Jenny said. "My cousin, Mr. Gunn, is the most loyal man I ever knew, and he fought the English crown. I have heard rumors that some Americans would like to do the same. The House of Hanover is German, and so I can imagine many a good Englishman chafing under George's rule. Scotland certainly does. The thing that makes Hanson a traitor, as James Gunn put it, is the fact that his loyalty is all to *himself.* My mother once told me he would do anything for money."

"Well, we have money," Jane said simply. "Why don't we just give him some to flee to Jamaica?"

Everyone just looked at her, struck with the simplicity of the idea. "How could we trust him to keep his word?" John asked.

"That is simple," Thomas said, running ahead. "We would require him to leave in such a way as to burn all his boats. He would be a deserter, one who could not come back home. He already knows that too many people know about his connections to the French now, even if we cannot prove it this moment, and he knows that it is bound to come out sometime. He is probably feeling as stuck as we feel. And third, we could offer him the second portion of the money after he has gone, after he has burned his boats. We don't have to trust him—he would have to trust us, which he knows he can do."

And so it was decided, and that evening Thomas sat down to compose an unsigned letter to Hanson, outlining their plan and the reasons for it. They anticipated everything, or so they thought, but the one mistake they made was in the amount they offered him to disappear into the Caribbean. They had overestimated how much money it had taken to make him betray his country in the first place, and they offered him considerably more than that. The effect this had was that Hanson quickly concluded that he could take the first portion of the money offered him, take his revenge and not regret losing the second portion at all. He would have more gold in his purse than he had ever reckoned on in the beginning. That, and his growing hatred—it had even grown past his greed—would be satisfied.

The letter was delivered to Hanson at the governor's mansion, and the next day, he returned a note to Thomas on his daily visit to the governor saying that he was willing to make such an agreement. Thomas read the note, nodded his approval and that night wrote another unsigned letter on how they would make the transfer of the first payment. Hanson agreed to this also, as indicated by another note the following day.

But because Hanson was still in town, both Thomas and John had taken to wearing their cutlasses every day. This was taken as a mild eccentricity, and so only a few people teased them about it. "Expecting the French fleet to sail up the Bay, are ye?" said one friend of Thomas at the tobacco warehouse. "Any day now," said Thomas, grinning.

It was arranged with Hanson that Thomas would reserve a berth for "a friend" on an outgoing sloop for the Caribbean. Thomas would leave a package for him in his cabin, containing all that was promised in his first payment. The captain was a friend of Thomas, and so he could guarantee that nothing would be tampered with in that private cabin. When Hanson had arrived in Jamaica, he would present himself under his new name to a business associate of the Monroe family, and would receive the second installment. He could then make his way off to South America, or other more distant parts. Everything had come together, just as arranged, and the sloop was due to sail at high tide on that particular Friday evening, in a late Maryland spring.

Hanson told the captain of the sloop that he would be back before high tide, and he made his way up from the harbor in the gathering twilight, seeking his revenge. He had long ago found out where the Monroe's lived, and he made his way there carefully, taking the back way so that he was unlikely to meet anyone he knew. He came up on the house from the back, and peering through a side window, he saw that the Monroe's and Jenny were taking their dinner quietly. He thought he could execute his mayhem in just a few moments, make his way back to the ship and leave the magistrates in Annapolis with a few unsolved murders.

There was a covered walkway between the house and the kitchen, and Hanson waited behind a hedge until he saw the cook coming out of the house again, heading for the kitchen. Hanson stepped in the back door and made his way silently toward the dining room. He would have accomplished everything that he wanted, just as he wanted, if a young serving girl had not come around the corner of the back passage with a tray full of dirty dishes. She saw Hanson with his cutlass out, screamed and dropped the entire tray, dashing into a side room. Hanson dove for the door of the dining room, but by the time he got through that door both Thomas and John were standing with drawn swords. John was the closer of the two, and so Hanson took an overhand swing at him, with all his strength. John swung his cutlass with both hands and batted Hanson's blow away. John fell to one knee, and Hanson's sword had lodged in the lower wooden lip of the china hutch. He labored for a second to pull it away, but, by the time he was free, Thomas had made it around the other side of the table and challenged him. But by this time, John was on his feet again, sword in both hands. Hanson looked from one to the other and turned on his heel and fled. At the back door, he bowled over the cook, who was coming in with the bread pudding dessert. They both tumbled to the ground, and Hanson's left hand went into the pudding, burning him badly. Hanson

swore, jumped to his feet and dashed around the corner of the
house. Seconds after him, John, and then Thomas, were running with drawn swords.

They chased him past St. Anne's, and then down Maryland
Avenue. Coming to the place where Prince George's Street ran
down toward the harbor, Hanson hesitated for a moment and
then stopped, taking his stand there. He could not run to the
sloop because the Monroe's knew right where he was going
and could stop it from sailing. He had to fight here, kill Thomas
and John and then make his way to the sloop without being
discovered. His case was fast becoming desperate, and he
knew it. The street was mostly deserted, and so he turned for
the fight.

John arrived first, and Hanson—who was after all, a soldier—parried John's thrust easily and John's cutlass clattered
to the cobblestone street. Hanson then took a backslash at
John's head, but John dodged and the cutlass just grazed his
cheek. John had fallen backward on to the street, but by this
time, Thomas had run up, breathing heavily. John was by now
crawling on all fours toward his sword, and Thomas took
up a fencing stance in front of Hanson. He was a little more
experienced than John, and so the flashing swords between
them looked like more of a genuine swordfight. John found
his sword and, reaching up, felt his cheek. He realized he was
bleeding heavily. He staggered to his feet, moving toward his
father and Hanson, who were now going at it, hammer and

tongs. Suddenly Thomas lunged forward with a deep thrust, stumbled on one of the paving stones and fell to his knees. With that, John leapt forward with a shout, pulling his sword over his head like an axe blow. The violence of this unorthodox attack caught Hanson by surprise, and he parried clumsily and took a few steps backward. He recovered his footing and then turned to face John again.

But by this time, a small group of seamen, attracted by a noise familiar to them, boiled out the door of a nearby tavern and had gathered in a group of spectators behind Hanson. John was advancing toward him, bleeding heavily, but still remembering what his father had taught him about attacking. *Maintain the offensive*, he thought. His father had gotten back on his feet by this time and was just a step behind John. But one of the seamen in the crowd suddenly shouted at Hanson, and jumped at him with a drawn sword. Hanson turned in surprise, and the sailor and Hanson were suddenly in the thick of it, blows falling furiously. But the sailor was far better with a cutlass than either John or Thomas, and suddenly Hanson bent over violently. A thrust had gone home, and Hanson fell dead to the street.

John looked at the sailor in surprise. "Hullo, Curtis," he said.

Church Across the Water

THE GOVERNOR HAD BEEN DULY ASTONISHED when he was informed that Major Hanson was the spy. It was not necessary to produce the papers that proved he was a spy, largely because there were multiple witnesses of his un-provoked attack on the Monroe household. "Was he the assassin then?" the governor asked Thomas Monroe.

"Well, no," said Thomas. "that part of the story was, um, inaccurate."

"Well, sink me," said the governor, ignoring him. "An assassin! Fancy!" Thomas concluded that this was part of the story that had already made it into one of the governor's reports to London, and so he decided to drop it. The governor was well on his way to becoming a hero, and Thomas decided there was no point in trying to stop him.

The previous two Lord's Days, John and Jenny had gone to the Presbyterian meeting house at the edge of town, and John's parents had continued on at St. Anne's. But they had been talking about what they would do, just as Thomas had promised, and so a week after the death of Major Hanson, Thomas went and had a very painful interview with the vicar.

With regard to the meeting house, Jenny had remarked on how different this meeting was from what she was used to in Scotland. "The preacher here is on fire," she said to Thomas and Jane after her second visit there. He says he was trained in Mr. Tennent's log college. Have you heard of Mr. Tennant, Mr. Monroe?"

"Yes, I have," Thomas said. "He is a hothead, but I believe he is a good man despite that. And our vicar is a good man too, but he is the kind of good man around whom nothing ever happens. Mr. Tennant is the kind of good man around whom many things happen, most of them good." It was just after that exchange that Thomas Monroe had his visit with the vicar. And the vicar really was a kindly old man, and so he gave his right hand to Thomas upon their parting and promised to do what he could to minimize the scandal in the town after the news got out. And the news was sure to be scandalous. The Monroes were one of the preeminent families of Annapolis, and to have them become *Presbyterian* was hard for that society to fathom.

And apparently, it was just as hard for the Presbyterians. The following Sunday, there was a great stir at the meeting house when the entire Monroe family showed up. Jane Monroe had debated whether to change how she dressed for worship since they were now going to divine services in a stable, but then decided that that would be the wrong thing to do. She was not sure why, but she was sure that it would be wrong somehow. One of the elders, a kindly gentleman, had greeted them at the door and offered them the bench in the front, but Thomas shook his head and said that they would prefer the back. After they had taken their seats, the elder came back to them and leaned over and whispered something in Thomas' ear. Thomas nodded, gratefully, and the two shook hands. "What did he say?" whispered Jane.

"He sought my forgiveness and said that he has read the epistle from James as well," Thomas said.

The order of service was unusual to the Monroes, who were accustomed to the prayer book, but the service was still simple, and so they got along well enough. The psalms were Genevan, not Anglican chants, but they were robustly sung, and Jane particularly liked how the psalms moved. "Almost like a jig," she said later. "And the harmonies are lovely. And the people sing like they are glad to be singing."

When the minister stepped up behind the simple wooden pulpit, he gathered his texts as though they were the reins of a horse, and he began to ride, vigorously. His name was Mr. Wyatt, and he preached very thoroughly, effectively and well. He was certainly not as great an orator as Mr. Whitefield, but what he said was nevertheless piercing and convicting. When Thomas and Jane talked about it later, the only thing they regretted was how long they had taken to make the decision. "But at the same time," Thomas told her, "these Presbyterians have the old Adam in them, too, and we can never think that we will ever go anywhere where there is no sin, no failing. Just think of what poor Jenny came from. It seems that the name *Presbyterian* is not a sufficient shield. After a while new wineskins will always turn into old wineskins."

The most striking thing about the service is what happened to John in the course of it. This was his third visit, and so he was not struck as much by the quality of the preaching as his parents were, but rather by how he had come full circle. He sat quietly, listening to Mr. Wyatt, just as he had listened to Mr. Whitefield out at sea. The preacher was across the water then, and just in front of Mr. Wyatt was a small baptismal font, directly in front of the pulpit. He was hearing the word from across the water again. He needed to hear the word in terms of the water. And so again, he checked his heart to see if he was starting to take pride in how well he understood that we ought not to take pride in anything. Mr. Wyatt's text was that it is not of him "that willeth, or him that runneth, but of God that sheweth mercy." John smiled to himself. *It is not of him that understandeth that it is not of him that willeth.* He was content, and divine sovereignty finally made sense to him—and precisely because he ceased trying to make sense of it in a way that he could take credit for.

There were about a hundred congregants there, and the service lasted for about two hours. The people were warm and friendly and excited. "It is interesting to meet them all here," Mr. Monroe said. "I know most of them from business in the town, and they are all the people that I enjoy working with the most. I don't think that is a coincidence."

After services, Thomas and Jane Monroe spent a long time speaking with Mr. Wyatt on the cobblestone street outside. Mr. Monroe had a long list of questions that they worked through, and when they were done, Thomas looked at Jane, sighed gratefully, and asked Mr. Wyatt if they could become members of his congregation. "You may," Mr. Wyatt said, "after I and one of my elders call upon you. We have some questions for you as well. But judging from our conversation thus far, I believe the results of that interview will be most satisfactory."

After the family got home from church, while the servants were preparing the food, John asked Jenny if she would take a walk with him around Church Circle. She agreed, surprised, but she also noticed the knowing glance that Thomas and Jane gave one another. Her immediate assumption was that she had done something terrible, and she had offended John's mother, and that John was going to have to tell her about it. She would be banished from this wonderful home, and she had no idea what she could possibly do after that. Beyond her control, tears came to her eyes. She was sure that her manners had been somehow offensive, or she had said something horrible without meaning to, and that she had wrecked everything. She had thought that this would happen.

As soon as they made it outside the house, she began. "John, I am very sorry ..."

John stared at her blankly. "For what?"

"I am not in trouble with your family?"

"Trouble?" John laughed out loud. "The only one in trouble will be me if I come back with the wrong answer."

Now it was Jenny's turn to stare blankly. "Wrong answer?"

John was not looking at her directly and seemed to be taking great interest in his shoes. After a moment, he finally raised his head and said, "Look here. Let me explain something that I noticed in church today. The minister preaches the same gospel as Mr. Whitefield does. He preaches it with the same fire. He is a different man, so the fire burns differently, but the fire is there. A pine log and an oak log burn very differently, but the fire is the same."

Jenny nodded. "Yes. That is very true."

"The first time I ever heard anyone preach that way was Mr. Whitefield himself when we were out at sea. I was thinking about that today while looking at Mr. Wyatt. Just as we looked at Mr. Whitefield preaching across the water, and heard his words as they echoed off the water, in the same way, I thought about hearing Mr. Wyatt with his words echoing off my baptism."

Jenny stared at John, amazed. "That is a wonderful way to think about it."

"And do you remember what I confessed to you after Curtis thrashed me so badly? That I had understood Mr. Whitefield saying that we could not be proud of grace, and I was proud of how I understood that?"

Jenny nodded. "I remember that, too."

"When Mr. Wyatt was preaching, I finally understood that God is God whether we understand it or not, and grace is grace whether we understand it or not, and I understood finally in a way that built me up—instead of puffing me up."

They continued to walk along quietly for a short time. Jenny was thinking about what he had said. John was silent for the moment because his tongue had suddenly swelled up and filled his entire mouth. But he finally managed to say, "And so I decided in church this morning, that to finish all the parallels, I now have to fall backwards off the ship and into the water. And I have to do it in a way that embarrasses me in front of you. So, then, there it is."

Jenny was bewildered. "*What* are you talking about?"

"Would you be willing to marry me? But I would really understand if you didn't want to."

James Gunn at Susan Creek

JAMES GUNN GOT OFF HIS SHIP IN BALTIMORE, but he knew that John and Jenny had sailed for Annapolis. Back in Glasgow, after *The Golden Sextant* sold to an English merchant, he had tried to get a berth on a ship for Annapolis but was unsuccessful in this, and so within a few days, he decided to sail to Baltimore instead and make his way down to Annapolis by coach.

When he arrived in Annapolis, he asked around industriously and was finally given directions to the Monroe house. Standing on the front walk outside that house, he whistled under his breath, and said, "Well, I dinna know if they've treated her right." He undid the latch to the gate and walked up to the front door muttering to himself. "I should have come with them. I should have just let the *Sextant* go."

The servant who answered the door bowed graciously and ushered James Gunn into the parlor. "May I say who is calling?" he inquired politely. After receiving the information, the servant made his way to the back of the house, and Mr. Gunn sat nervously on the edge of one of the seats. After just a few minutes, there was a bustle from the rear of the house, and Jenny soon burst in, followed by Jane Monroe. "Oh, it is wonderful to see you!" Jenny exclaimed, throwing her arms around his neck. "We have had such adventures! Well, John mostly."

Letting him go, Jenny then introduced him to Mrs. Monroe. "This is John's mother. And she is going to be my mother-in-law next month."

James Gunn's eyebrows went up in mock seriousness. "And ye dinna ask me?"

"Oh, we would have if you had been here, you old dear. Or maybe we wouldn't have. It took everything John had to ask just *one* person." They all laughed, and as Thomas and John came into the room just then, they had to explain the joke. John laughed with them, but later it occurred to him that earlier he might have been annoyed at something like that—and wondered briefly why he hadn't been.

Thomas and James shook hands and took an instant liking to one another. They all sat down in the parlor and recounted all that had happened to them since they had parted. "Curtis, eh?" said Mr. Gunn. "I have thrown him out of *The Golden*

Sextant at least three times. The last time was the hardest, and it took me at least ten minutes. That is part of what convinced me I had to get out of the tavern trade. The only worst fighting I ever did was at Culloden. I am glad that scapegrace has done something to get back in my good graces."

Eventually the conversation turned to what Mr. Gunn was planning to do in the New World. He had money from the sale of his tavern that he could use to establish himself, he knew how to manage a business, and he wanted to get as far away from the English crown as possible. "Without getting too close to the French crown," he added. "I am beginning to grow allergic to crowns, Bonnie Prince or no Bonnie Prince."

At that, Thomas's eyes lit up. "Aye, then I'll take you to see the governor tomorrow then."

"Why is that?"

"After Hanson was killed, it was revealed that his contact was Mr. Delacroix at Susan Creek. Delacroix owned and ran a very profitable business there with the trappers, and so the royal governor seized all his possessions after all his intriguing was uncovered. So I suppose Delacroix will just have to stay in Quebec. But the colony does not really want to own this business—I would be happy to introduce you to the governor as one who wants to buy it. The governor was just asking me about this yesterday. He will think I am a superb counselor to show up with a buyer just two days later."

James Gunn laughed out loud at this and asked a host of

questions about where it was and how much money it would take to buy, most of which Thomas was able to answer. But what settled it for him was the realization that he would not be that far from where John and Jenny were to be living. "Aye, I'll do it then," he said. "Unless the governor makes me kiss his foot."

"You wouldn't actually have to kiss his foot," Jenny said. "When I was over there, he was wearing silk slippers."

"Agghh," James Gunn said. "That is why I am growing weary of these effete changelings. Silk, perfume, periwigs and all the rest of it. This place I am buying—is the water clean? Is the air good? Do the bears wear silk slippers?"

Thomas Monroe nodded. "There's many here in America that share that sentiment, I'll assure you. I have merchant friends who travel to London regularly. Most of them think it is like Sodom. The rest think it is more like Gomorrah."

"There'll be trouble across the water from that, I warrant you. Good believers are coming over here from Scotland in the tens of thousands, and I hear there's even more coming from Ulster. Can two walk together unless they be agreed? That's what the book says."

"Aye," said Thomas. "There's trouble brewing. Most don't see it, but I certainly do."

Three years later, John and Jenny Monroe were visited at their estate by James Gunn, who had become a very prosperous merchant indeed. He had helped to establish the Presbyterian Church at Susan Creek, and he was one of the ruling elders there. He agreed with Jenny about creaky preachers and helped to ensure that their pulpit was the most vigorous place in the county. "Give me a revival man every time. I want a minister who spits on his hands before he preaches," he said.

John had learned a lot from his father, and, while he agreed that there was nothing worse than dead preaching, he replied to Mr. Gunn with only, "Well, I'm not sure it is all that simple."

But still, they had a wonderful visit. They had a grand veranda that wrapped around the house, and the Monroes and James Gunn were sitting there in early evening, in the summer of 1750. They were largely done talking and were all just enjoying themselves as they watched the heir of the house, two-year-old William Monroe, staggering heroically across the grass. He had his small breeches stuffed with twigs and acorns, which he would periodically throw at a bird, or a leaf on the ground, or at nothing in particular.

William had only just learned about his offensive capabilities. Two days before, a chattering squirrel had caused him to beat a hasty retreat back to his mother. But his father had come out of the house, stooped down, talked with him for a moment, and passed on what *his* father had taught to him. "Whenever there is doubt, always attack. Always move forward. Don't let him see you afraid."

"He doesn't understand all that, John," Jenny had said.

"He understands enough of it. And I am sure I will be reminding him again soon enough."

And so it was, that evening when John and Jenny and James were sitting on the front porch watching William enjoy his grassy empire, that a small terrier came around the corner of the house.

Jenny stood up immediately. "Is that the Hastings' terrier?" she asked. "Is he friendly?"

John leaned forward and was ready to move if he needed to. "Let's see," he said.

A moment later, William caught sight of the dog and hesitated a few seconds. He then looked around at his father, saw that he was there, turned back toward the dog and charged. Which is exactly the same thing that he did years later in the American War for Independence—in the great sea battle between the *Serapis* and the *Bon Homme Richard.*

But that, I am afraid, is another story.

About the Author

Douglas Wilson is the pastor of Christ Church, Moscow, Idaho, and author of numerous books including *Recovering the Lost Tools of Learning*, not to mention a collection of books on marriage and parenting. His previous contribution to this series was *Blackthorn Winter.*